Joey and the "What If" Bubbles

by Kathleen D. Mitchell

Copyright © 2015 Kathleen D. Mitchell.

All rights reserved. No part of this book may be used or reproduced by any means, graphic, electronic, or mechanical, including photocopying, recording, taping or by any information storage retrieval system without the written permission of the publisher except in the case of brief quotations embodied in critical articles and reviews.

WestBow Press books may be ordered through booksellers or by contacting:
WestBow Press
A Division of Thomas Nelson & Zondervan
1663 Liberty Drive
Bloomington, IN 47403
www.westbowpress.com
1 (866) 928-1240

Because of the dynamic nature of the Internet, any web addresses or links contained in this book may have changed since publication and may no longer be valid. The views expressed in this work are solely those of the author and do not necessarily reflect the views of the publisher, and the publisher hereby disclaims any responsibility for them.

Illustrations © Linda Pierce.

ISBN: 978-1-4908-6070-1 (sc)
ISBN: 978-1-4908-6071-8 (e)

Library of Congress Control Number: 2014920755

Printed in the United States of America.

WestBow Press rev. date: 1/30/2015

This book is dedicated to my precious grandchildren ...

Devin Douglas ... Aviel David ... Graham Patrick ...

Claire Rosa ... Lydia Yael ...

and to the little ones yet to be born.

I pray that each of these children ...

and all of those, who read this book ...

will know the One, who transforms all our scary **what ifs**

into glorious opportunities for overcoming.

Joey Aiken was like any other adventurous 8-year-old boy. He loved hanging from tree branches and catching frogs in the stream behind his house. He could ride his bicycle backwards around the block, as easily as he could dribble a soccer ball down field to make a score. He loved telling silly jokes, and usually laughed louder than everyone else at the punch line. Everyone in his class at school knew that Joey could burp louder than anyone for miles around. On really hot days he would stuff his mouth with chocolate ice cream until he could feel his brain begin to freeze. Joey was fearless and so much fun ... that is until one day last September. Something strange happened to Joey that day.

On September 12th, Joey began to worry. It happened without warning. There he was, confidently sitting at his table in the school lunchroom at high noon; crunching happily on a piece of garlic bread. In the next minute, a loud crash was heard echoing throughout the dining hall. A deafening roar, of many children laughing hysterically, immediately followed that sudden crash, as if a circus clown had just entered the room. Looking around, Joey saw his friend Peter standing in a puddle of milk with spaghetti sauce and noodles splattered all over his feet and legs. Somehow Peter's tray had slipped out of his hands as he was walking toward the table to join Joey for lunch. Now Peter was standing in the middle of the lunchroom, empty-handed, wearing his lunch all over himself, with everyone staring and laughing at him. His face showed his embarrassment, as his cheeks took on the color of a bright, ripe, tomato. The blush of red on his face actually matched the sauce that now covered his shoes. Somewhere, way down within Joey, there was the tiniest bit of a laugh trying to pop of out of his mouth; but something made it stick there inside his stomach. What was his friend feeling in this moment of unhappy attention?

Out of the blue, Joey began to feel queasy in his stomach as a horrifying thought jumped into his mind. "What if that had been ME instead of Peter?

What if I had dropped MY tray and splattered spaghetti everywhere? What if everyone was laughing at ME right now? What if I was the person standing in the middle of the lunchroom with nothing to eat, while noodles hung helplessly from my jeans?" Those were horrifying thoughts for Joey.

Throughout the afternoon, he just kept thinking about that embarrassing scene. He could hardly wait to get home to find comfort in the security of his own bedroom. There, in that safe, quiet, space, he had many things to distract him from these scary thoughts. Maybe in his bedroom, surrounded by his toys, and focused on his video games, he could erase those lunchroom memories.

Only once before in his whole life, had Joey witnessed that kind of humiliation in school. Oh, yes, it was GROSS

humiliation for Jennifer Klein, when she didn't make it to the bathroom, before she threw up in the middle of the hallway last year. Kids talked about that stinky event for several days.

Oh, how Joey wanted to run home and close the door on this whole lunchroom fiasco! Finally, the last bell rang. Without stopping by his locker to pick up his jacket, Joey sprinted toward home with the speed of a professional baseball player rounding third base on the way to home plate. Once inside the door of his house, Joey barely paused to snag a glass of milk and a cookie before retreating to the safety of his room. Slamming the door shut with his foot, while trying hard to keep his milk from spilling, Joey finally felt as if he could breathe a sigh of relief. It felt so good to nibble on his cookie and to slurp his milk in this familiar, quiet, place, where he could finally be alone. He kicked off his shoes, and settled back on his comfy bed to relax. When the last sip of milk was swallowed down, and the final morsel of cookie gobbled up, Joey tucked his hands behind his head and happily sank into his pillow. Today was passing away, and a new and brighter day was coming tomorrow.

    Joey was holding that thought in his mind, when, just for one tiny second, the scene in the lunchroom jumped back into his head ... complete with full color images and surround sound. Why couldn't he just forget about all that? Then, the truth of his fear came out into the open. With a shaky voice Joey closed his eyes tightly and said out loud, "Ohhhh, what if I had been the one who dropped my tray today? That would have been soooo TERRIBLE!!!"

At that exact moment, when Joey spoke those words out loud, a very strange thing happened.

It all started when Joey faintly heard a quiet sort of groaning sound above his head. When he opened his eyes to see what that strange noise was all about, Joey was startled to find that there was a very large, transparent, bubble floating just above his head. This was not an ordinary bubble like those he often blew out of soap solution. This bubble was huge and was yellowy green. It was a little bigger than his soccer ball. Not knowing what to do, Joey blinked his eyes; trying to decide if he was imagining this floating thing. Should he try to touch it? What was it, and where did it come from? Deciding to see if it was real and if he could pop it, Joey poked his pointer finger at the bubble. It felt kind of smushy and stretchy, but didn't break.

At first the bubble didn't move, but then, as if it had a mind of its own, it floated upward and out of reach. Joey watched it bounce along the ceiling for a while, until it settled into the corner just above his dresser. That's where the mysterious bubble decided to stay.

To be absolutely certain that he was not dreaming or imagining the bubble, Joey threw his shoe at it. The shoe just bounced off the bubble and flew back toward his head. That settled it! This strange thing was real. YOIKS!! What was he to do now? Considering if the bubble was dangerous or harmless, Joey decided he would just watch it for a while to see it if eventually popped, like regular bubbles do. It didn't pop. It just stayed in the corner of his ceiling, as if it was perfectly happy to be there.

As time passed his curiosity got the best of him. Joey decided to take a closer look with his spy kit binoculars. He didn't want to get too close to the bubble, so he stood on his bed and focused in on it from there. Looking through the binoculars revealed something really interesting about this strange bubble. Joey could see that there were two words bumping around inside it. Maybe it had a name or a message locked in there. Focusing his binoculars on the assembled letters, Joey clearly read two words ...

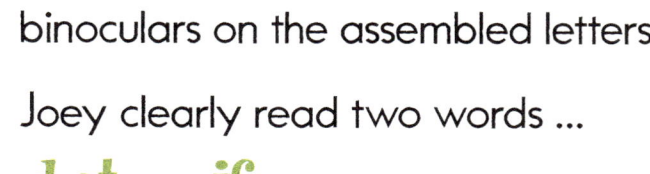

what and **if**.

Deciding that the bubble might be

an unusual sort of pet for him ... something quite harmless ... he decided to keep it without telling anyone about it. He wouldn't have to feed it or clean up after it. But keeping this bubble had to be a secret. If other people knew about it, they might try to take it or to pop it. For some strange reason, this odd bubble felt comfortable to Joey. He rather liked it, so he decided to leave it alone to see what would happen.

Dinnertime came and went without anyone in the family knowing his private secret. Not wanting to raise suspicion, Joey studied his spelling words and watched a little TV as usual that evening; checking every so often to see if the bubble was still in his room. Yup! The bubble was still there at bedtime, hiding in the dark shadow of the corner. It was still there when Joey left for school in the morning.

As Joey entered his classroom, he was reminded that it was the day for the big spelling competition in the third grade! Joey had always been great in spelling, but while he was waiting for the 1 o'clock event to start, he began to feel a bit strange in his stomach. To Joey, the minutes seemed to be ticking by too quickly as the hour moved toward the big spelling challenge. By the time it was his turn to spell, Joey had nervous feelings crawling all over his body. He began to have worried thoughts like: "What if my mind suddenly forgets every word I ever learned?" "**What if** my brain spells one way, and my mouth says something else?" Just as the teacher was about to give Joey his first word to spell, the fire drill alarm sounded. Everyone had to immediately stop what he or she was doing, and practice walking safely outside the building. It was the rule! Whew! Joey was so grateful to be saved by that fire drill.

While he was standing silently in line with his classmates on the sidewalk, waiting for the fire drill to end, Joey had several more worrisome thoughts pop into his mind. "**What if** this wasn't a drill? What if the school really IS on fire?" "How often do schools catch on fire?" While he was still considering these troubling questions, Joey got some good news. The fire drill was ended, and the spelling competition was being postponed until tomorrow, because of the interruption.

Relieved that his school day had ended without anything bad happening, Joey scampered home, eager to see if that odd bubble was still floating in the corner of his room. As he opened his bedroom door and rushed in, Joey got quite a surprise! There was not just one bubble floating around, there were three more yellowy, green bubbles, drifting around the ceiling in the company of the first one! What should he do now? After giving the situation some serious thought, Joey decided that these funny bubbles were most interesting, so he wouldn't bother them ... and he certainly wouldn't tell his parents about them. The way his mother liked his room to be clean, she would definitely sweep them out if she knew they were there. Joey wasn't at all sure that he wanted these strange bubbles to go away.

Every day, throughout the whole week, Joey's collection of bedroom bubbles grew. Two appeared during breakfast on Wednesday, when Joey began to worry about Megan's birthday party. They showed up in his room when he said,

"Mom, I really like Megan, but what if she doesn't invite me to her party next week? What if I get to go, but then she doesn't like my present?"

Five more bubbles met him in his room on Thursday after Joey returned from the soccer game. Joey's worries about the game had popped out of his mouth while he was strapping on his shin guards and lacing up his shoes.

"What if the other team is a lot better than us?"

"What if I get turned around

and kick the ball toward the wrong goal by mistake? I saw that happen at a game a couple of weeks ago. Everyone on the field howled with laughter as the member of the other team, added a point to our score."

"What if, my coach keeps me on the bench most of the game?"

"What if, my Dad doesn't come in time to see me play?"

"What if we loose and don't get into the big tournament?"

More what if questions were pouring into his mind every minute.

Wherever he was, every time Joey spoke out a worried "what if," a new bubble would appear in his bedroom. On Friday, when his friend Avery came down with the chickenpox, four more bubbles appeared.

"**What if** I get Avery's chickenpox?"

"**What if** I don't get to finish my Cub Scout project because I'm home sick in bed?"

"**What if** the chickenpox makes me look bumpy on my face like that other kid in third grade?"

"**What if** I already have chickenpox in my body, and don't know it?"

By the time Friday evening came, Joey's room was very crowded with **what if** bubbles. It was becoming very difficult for him to squeeze into his room and to crawl around underneath them. When the sun came up on Saturday morning, Joey began to wonder what would happen, if he could no longer open and close his bedroom door. "What if I get trapped in here for my whole life?" With those words, another bubble appeared right before his eyes.

Joey was in the habit of worrying about almost everything by now. He didn't know how to stop. "What if I stay short and never grow tall?" "What if my scout campout next week gets rained out, so that I can't finish my hiking badge?" "What if I forget to close the cage door tightly and my gerbil gets out of his cage, so that I can't find him again?" "What if my cousin Aaron looses the video game he borrowed from me? That game is my favorite!"

It was getting to the point that Joey was spending most of his time in the bedroom, with the whole bubble mess becoming too much for him to handle. Absolutely no one was allowed to come into his room for fear that the bubbles would be discovered. The very day that the first bubble appeared, Joey had taped a sign to his door saying, "PRIVATE ...STAY OUT!! As a result of that sign, no one but Joey knew about what was going on just inside his door.

He knew that something had to be done, but Joey had

absolutely no idea how to get rid of those bubbles. They weren't fun or interesting any more. They were becoming a big problem. Those crazy bubbles had become pests that wouldn't go away. That fearful thought just added to Joey's bubble problem, when he said, "What if these bubbles never leave and never pop?" BOINK! Just that quickly, another bubble appeared in the room.

Joey had tried everything he could think of to make the bubbles go away. He had opened his window, hoping that they would fly out. They didn't float away. He tried stuffing them into his closet, but they wouldn't stay there. Hitting them with his baseball bat didn't help at all. These things were becoming a big, crowded, mess in his room! How could he keep this secret much longer? Should he continue to keep the secret?

Just as Joey was about to loose all hope, he heard a knock on his door late Saturday afternoon. "Oh, no!" he thought. With a shaky voice, Joey said, "Who is it?" A gentle, familiar, voice answered his nervous question.

"Joey, this is Grandpa Zach. Can I come in to see you?"

"No, Grandpa ... not today," Joey responded.

"Well, Joey, the fact is, I need your help today ... right now. Can I please come in to see you?"

"I don't know if you can, Grandpa", Joey whispered.

"Why not son?" said Grandpa.

"The room is too crowded in here."

"Well, what if I try to come in and help you clean it out a bit?"

That was all Joey needed to hear! He was tired of all these bothersome **what ifs**. His mind and his world were getting so overcrowded with them, that he couldn't even play anymore. Maybe Grandpa Zach really

could help. As Joey forced open the door, Grandpa Zach peeked in.

"Ahhh ... I see it IS a bit tight in your room, Joey. No worries ... I can squeeze in."

Maybe it was because Joey knew he really needed help. Maybe it was because Grandpa Zach wasn't shocked or angry to see all the bubbles in his room. Whatever it was, suddenly Joey felt so much better knowing that his secret was now shared with someone who loved him. Even with all those big bubbles pressing down, Grandpa Zach still had enough room to gather Joey into his arms and give him a big, warm, hug.

"So, Joey, tell me about these bubbles. Where did they come from?" Grandpa asked. Joey whispered quietly, "I guess we could call them **what if** bubbles, because that is what is written inside them. Every time I say '**What If**?' another one appears."

"Joey, have lots of things been worrying you lately? Have you been feeling afraid that things might not work out well in your day?"

"I guess so, Grandpa. At first nothing seemed to bother me. But when I started thinking about things going on, or things that might happen ... things that I couldn't stop, fix, or change, these bubbles began to appear.

Some of my worries seemed kind of silly at first, but as I thought about them more, they also began to sound scary to me. I just don't want to have bad things happen, Grandpa! And I really don't want people to laugh at me or not like me. I don't want to mess up and make mistakes."

"Well, Joey, nobody wants bad things to happen, but most of the time, when they do, there are ways to fix them, or to make things better. Nobody likes to mess up or to fail at something, but at some time ALL of us have that happen. We just might need someone to help us deal with those things. Often the stuff we worry about never happens at all. But, when uncomfortable things do happen, you need to know that we can deal with those things together. You and I, and others, who love you, can deal with the fear of bad things too. Together we can make changes, and together we can work through hurts and problems. Sometimes we just need to put our brains and our prayers together to get to the solutions, and to get back to the truth. So tell me about these **what if** worries you have stored in this room?"

It was then that Joey began to tell Grandpa Zach everything. He listed every **what if** and told Grandpa what was happening when each bubble appeared. After the whole story was told, Joey asked, "What do I do now to get rid of all these **what if** bubbles? They just NEVER pop!"

"Oh, yes ... they DO pop", Grandpa Zach declared "The best

way to pop a **what if** is to think past it, and then zap it with a **so what if**. Do you want to give it a try?" Grandpa pointed his finger at one of the bubbles and said, "**so what if** you drop your tray in the lunchroom and people laugh. You can clean up the mess and get another tray. You might even want to laugh at yourself for wearing spaghetti. After all, the laughter won't last long, and the accident will soon be forgotten. Now, you point your finger at that bubble over there in the corner like I did, and say **so what if**!"

Joey did exactly as Grandpa Zach told him to do, and POP, the first bubble disappeared. "So what if I miss a spelling word or forget one, I am still a great speller, who maybe needs to practice a little bit more." Joey pointed his finger at another bubble and said out loud, "So what if I don't win in the spelling competition, I can still spell lots of words and will study to learn more." Instantly that bubble popped.

On and on they went; zapping each bubble with a "**so what if**."

"**so what if** the school really has a fire one day. All the successful drills will keep the children safe, and the firemen that come to the school are trained to put out fires". POP! "**so what if** I get chickenpox. Grandpa always visits me while I am sick, and mom says that I will never get chickenpox again once I have had them." POP!

Finally, after about an hour of calling out **so what ifs**, the last bubble was gone and Joey's room was back to normal. It felt so good for Joey to walk and jump and run around his room again. Happily climbing up on his grandpa's lap, Joey asked one more question. "Grandpa, if both big people and little people, old people and young people, can have problems with **what ifs**, how do <u>you</u> keep **what if** bubbles from happening to YOU?" "The best thing I know to do, Joey, is understand that there is someone bigger than all of the problems and scary things in the whole world. We don't need to worry about what might happen. The Creator, who made us, knows that we are too little and too scared to handle our big problems by ourselves; so He takes care of the really big things, and helps us know how to take care of the smaller things. We don't have to know all the answers, and we don't ever have to be alone; keeping scary things a secret. Difficult things can make us stronger. Getting help from other people can remind us that we have important things to share with each other, and that we are made to help each other, as we bless and need the Creator.

And knowing that SOMEONE REALLY BIG and POWERFUL LOVES US, knows our fears, and is here to help us, keeps many of those "what ifs" from crowding out our lives, and from taking our joy. Now that you know how to zap those nasty what ifs, I think you will be able to help other people learn to zap them too. And that is a very good thing, to come from all this bubble mess ... don't you think?"

"Yup, I think so, Grandpa. Thanks a lot! so what if you and I go out right now, to get some ice cream TOGETHER?"

"Now that's a worry-free "what if" that I know we can handle together, Joey! Let's do it!"

And from that afternoon until now, Joey never again had a what if bubble hanging around his room. Every bubble that occasionally appeared was immediately zapped with his so what if words and with his pointing finger. Instead of worrying, Joey practiced his spelling words and his soccer skills, and he grew and grew until he was the tallest one in his class. He always held on tightly to his lunch tray, but laughed out loud, if his own glass of milk tipped over; making everyone at his table laugh along with him. To this day, Joey is often the one, who laughs the loudest, when he accidently messes up. He understands that each of his small mistakes are covered by a **so what if**, and that each one can be an opportunity for him to learn something important. But most of all, Joey understands, in the middle of his heart, that the unconditional love of SOMEONE BIGGER than everyone, and GREATER than every problem, is willing and able handle the **what ifs** that might pop up.

CPSIA information can be obtained
at www.ICGtesting.com
Printed in the USA
LVOW06s2332030417
529477LV00004BA/4/P